GU00731269

MILO

AND THE

DRAGONS

PHIL HAMPTON

Illustrated by Rosie Quinn Harley

Copyright © Phil Hampton, 2022

All rights reserved. No part of this book may be reproduced or used in any manner without written permission of the copyright owner except for the use of quotations in a book review.

First paperback edition May 2022

Cover design and illustrations by
Rosie Quinn Harley

ISBN: 9798830830393

Dedicated to my wonderful grandson, Inti,
who was the inspiration for this book.

Table of Contents

CHAPTER ONE

Our adventure begins at 4 o'clock on a hot sunny day in July. It was so hot that you could lay a slice of bread onto the tarmac in the playground and turn it into toast. Milo knew this because he'd tried it at lunchtime with one of the slices from his peanut butter sandwich, and it had worked. He wished it hadn't though, because the peanut butter had started to bubble and gurgle in the heat until it looked like a big gloopy lump of baby poo, and then he really didn't want to eat it anymore.

When the bell rang for the end of school, Milo grabbed his bag from the hook and raced home as fast as he could. Every day after school, and almost every weekend, he would play football in the field with his best friend Edwood. He would have preferred to have gone straight there but his mum always wanted him to do his chores before he was allowed out to play. Sometimes she told him to make his bed or clean his school shoes. Worst of all was when he had to tidy his room.

As Milo flung open the front door, he hoped his mum didn't have too much work for him to do. "I'm home!" he called out, dumping his schoolbag at the bottom of the stairs. "Can I go to the field now?"

Milo's mum walked through from the kitchen into the hallway, covered in flour. "Hello, love. Did you have a good day?" she said, with a big smile on her face. But her smile didn't last very long. "What on earth is that?" She stepped towards Milo and lowered her head until her frizzy red curls - the same colour as Milo's - were almost touching his nose. "Is that peanut butter?" she said, her finger pointing at a big brown splodge on the front of his school shirt.

Milo nodded. He didn't want to tell her how Edwood had picked up their newly made 'playground toast' and had tried to shove it into Milo's mouth, and nor how they had ended up having a sandwich fight, which Edwood had won when he'd lobbed a tomato at him.

"And what's this red stuff?" she said, pointing at another glob of mess.

"It's tomato juice," Milo said quietly. "Can I go the park now? Pleeease, Mum?"

She shook her head and looked a little bit sangry (which is half way between sad and angry). "Why do you find it so hard to get your food into your mouth, Milo?" she said with a sigh. "You're nine-years-old! You should be able to eat properly by now!"

Milo looked up at her with his big brown eyes, opened them up as wide as he could and gave her the sweetest smile. He didn't say another word, even though he wanted to ask her how *she* had managed to get covered in so much flour. He just waited ... and waited ... and blinked a few times, smiling more and more, until his cheeks were about to burst, and then his mum said, "Oh, go on then. But make sure you get back before it gets dark, and watch yourself crossing the road, and don't talk −"

"...to strangers," Milo finished, tugging off his school shoes to put on his favourite blue trainers.

Milo didn't have any brothers or sisters so he was used to doing a lot of things on his own, but he really liked playing with Edwood. The best thing of all was that Edwood only lived across the road, in the same street. If they both stood at their bedroom windows they could wave to each other, or make silly faces at each other, which they did nearly every night before they went to sleep.

Milo closed his front door, walked to the edge of the kerb and looked left, right, and left again, and then crossed the road to the other side, worrying a little bit about whether he should have looked right first instead of left. But he got there safely and within seconds he was prodding his finger onto Edwood's doorbell.

However, instead of feeling happy and excited, Milo suddenly felt a little bit strange. His tummy started to gurgle, which made him think of baby poo sandwiches, and then he started to feel a little bit sick.

The thing is, after the whole pavement toast thing, and after Edwood had lobbed half his packed lunch and a tomato at him, they'd had an argument.

A really BIG argument...

...About dragons.

cHApTER TWO

While Milo was still worrying about whether or not he'd crossed the road properly, he started to worry about whether Edwood would actually open the door. Milo worried about things *a lot*. He often wondered what would happen if the sun fell out of the sky, as he was afraid of the dark. But before he had time to worry too much about it actually happening, the door swung open and Edwood appeared on the doorstep.

"Hi," Milo said.

"Hi," Edwood said.

And everything felt really, *really* awkward.

"Do you want to come and play football?" Milo asked, looking at his friend.

Edwood had blond hair to match his ice blue eyes, which sometimes made it seem as if he was staring at you when really he was only listening as hard as he could, but even so, Milo looked away. He'd noticed that Edwood was wearing a new football kit and wanted to ask who had bought it for him, but he didn't.

"Are you coming then?" Milo said, with his fingers crossed behind his back.

"Okay then," Edwood said, and they headed off to the field.

They'd only kicked the ball back and forth a few times when Edwood started to talk about dragons again. Edwood always claimed he knew FAR more about dragons than Milo did, and that's what had started the argument at lunchtime, when he'd told Milo precisely what dragons like to eat, which was meat, apparently.

"The dragons stole some sheep from the farm over there last month," Edwood said, pointing into the distance while dribbling the ball between his feet. "And they stole some sea lions from the zoo as well."

"That's all rubbish," Milo said. "It would have been in the news, and nobody has heard a thing about it."

"Ah, but it's all top secret. My dad is a scientist and studies dragons at the university. He gets to know *everything* about dragons."

"You're making it up," Milo said, beginning to feel a little bit cross.

"No I'm not!" Edwood yelled. "The flames coming out of their nostrils are 369 thousand degrees Celsius, and their skin looks really rough but it's smooth. They all have purple eyes, and their tongues are always orange from the fire they breathe. And they have five rotten teeth…two on the right side and three on the left, and they stink!"

Milo didn't believe that Edwood knew more about dragons. He couldn't even spell his own name properly. Everyone knew that it was spelled EdWARD!

"I bet you didn't know that Wood Dragons eat wood, and they're called Wood Dragons because they eat people who have WOOD in their names!" Milo told him.

"That's not true. It's just not true!" Edwood said, suddenly stamping his foot on the ground and clenching his fist.

Milo had never seen Edwood so upset and angry, which made him feel a bit frightened, and he ran away. He ran and ran and ran until he couldn't see Edwood any more.

Milo had run so far he found himself lost in a field he didn't recognise. It was beginning to get dark and, as you know, he *hated* the dark. He hated it more than he hated spiders, and that was quite a lot. Although he had been annoyed with Edwood, he really wished his friend was there with him now. He'd been silly to tell him that stupid story about dragons eating people with WOOD in their name, he thought, because it wasn't true at all.

Hoping that it wasn't going to get dark too quickly, Milo looked at the sun and kept running towards it. He thought that if he ran as fast as he could he might stop it from sinking down under the horizon. But it soon disappeared and before long he found himself in darkness. He thought it would be a good idea if he stopped running altogether but before he could he suddenly crashed into something which was very big, very smooth and very, very hot. He bumped off it with a thwack! and was flung flat onto his back.

After a couple of seconds, and when the stars had stopped spinning around in his head, he felt his face becoming warmer and when he opened his eyes he saw a huge flame roar upwards into the sky, lighting up an ENORMOUS animal that he recognised as...

... A fully grown dragon!!!

cHAPTER THREE

Milo blinked a few times and then pinched himself to check if he was dreaming, but he wasn't. He peered up at the huge dragon, wishing the ground would just open up and swallow him. The dragon was mostly coloured green and yellow, had a long, muscular tail and a scaly body with feathers on its neck. It also had very bright eyes and two gigantic ears that twitched constantly. Its large claws were bright red and looked fearsomely sharp.

"Hello, dear boy," the dragon said, in a surprisingly soft voice. "Are you alright? You seemed to have run into me. Where have you come from? You were running very fast to get somewhere. Are you in trouble?"

Milo gulped and tried to catch his breath.

"I, I, I was uh… running away from my friend because I, I… was frightened he was going to attack me, but, uh… now I'm lost," he replied, now quite worried about being next to a big dragon who could make flames spurt out of its nostrils and could actually speak. He felt tiny next to this mammoth beast and he wished he was safe at home.

Another gigantic flame belched from the dragon and up into the sky, and Milo could clearly see the dragon's eyes, which weren't purple at all. In fact, one was blue and the other one was green.

"I knew Edwood was wrong," Milo muttered, feeling a little bit smug and superior. He couldn't wait to see Edwood's face when he told him, and that dragons can speak. He sat up and hugged his knees against his chest.

"What's your name, dear boy?" asked the dragon.

"Milo," Milo said. "What's yours?"

"I'm known as Mildred, although my real name is Lucia. I don't know why but it's always been that way."

"That's funny, to have two names," Milo said nervously. "But I suppose it's useful if you want to pretend you're a different dragon, eh?"

Mildred laughed. "Well, it's quite easy for me to go around unnoticed, but yes, if I get into trouble with one name I can always use the other."

Milo wondered how on earth a dragon of her size could get around and not been seen. Mildred was staring at him, waiting for him to speak, but he didn't know what else to say. She seemed kind, very polite and gentle, but could he trust her? He wasn't sure.

He was mulling this over when Mildred said, "Well, Milo, why was your friend trying to hurt you?"

He coughed and licked his lips. It felt as if the flames had taken all the moisture from the air. "We were arguing about who knew the most about dragons," he said, a little embarrassed. He told Mildred what he and Edwood had both said to each other.

A sad smile came across Mildred's long, wide dragon mouth. "I'm not sure that either of you know much about dragons," she said softly. "It seems silly to argue about something you don't know very much about. Do you think, perhaps, you should both have agreed to find out more about dragons together, rather than trying to outdo each other and be the best?"

Milo had to agree, and was thinking about how he could make it up with Edwood when his thoughts were interrupted again.

"Would you like me to tell you some *real* facts about dragons?" Mildred asked.

Milo sat up on the grass. "I'd like that very much!" he said with a grin.

CHAPTER four

Mildred peered down at Milo, her long eyelashes fluttering. "Do you know we speak every language in the world except Hungarian?" She shook her head slightly and Milo ducked to avoid one of her ears slapping him in the face. "We all agreed the language was far too difficult to learn. And here's another fact... dragons only come out at night. In the beginning we needed to have flames so we could see where we were going in the dark."

"I never thought of that," Milo replied. "What colour is your tongue?"

Mildred raised something that could have been an eyebrow, but Milo wasn't entirely sure. "Why do you want to know?"

"Well," Milo said, "my friend Edwood told me that all dragons' tongues are orange. It would be nice to be able to tell him if he was right or not."

"I can do better than just tell you," Mildred said. "I can *show* you. Do you want to see?"

Milo nodded slowly, still a little scared, and Mildred opened her mouth as wide as it could go and stuck out her tongue, which was twice as long as Milo, before flopping it onto the grass. It was as black as coal.

Edwood stared, wide-eyed. "Wow! Why is it so black?"

"Because the fire I breathe through my nostrils always burns it if I forget to open my mouth at the same time. But if I remember to open it I get lots of fresh air, which helps to cool it down. By the way, all dragons' tongues are green when they are born. Did you know that? Would you like to climb onto it and explore it?"

Milo wasn't sure what he should do. He was quite worried about making this decision. He wondered what his granddad, Sam, would do in this situation. Grandad Sam had told Milo many stories about when he'd had to make serious decisions in his life. Like, when he had to decide which path to take in the jungle in Africa when he was lost.

"Should I have taken the path that might have been full of lions or the one that could have been full of dragons?" he'd asked Milo.

Grandad Sam had decided on a path and, luckily for him, it was the lions' path and he survived. He was lucky because Grandad Sam knew a little about lions and *absolutely nothing* about dragons. He'd been told that if you were perfectly still, stood as tall as you could, raised your arms up and then waved them about wildly, lions didn't like it. Apparently, you should also yell at the top of your voice and never ever run. If you do this, lions will probably ignore you or, if they don't, you should throw anything you can find at them. If nothing else works you could try and bribe them with a jam sandwich from your rucksack, which is exactly what Grandad Sam did, and it worked.

Milo suddenly realised that Mildred was looking at him with her enormous eyes, waiting for a decision. "Won't I get burnt if I stand on your tongue?" he said, already forgetting Mildred's explanation. But he still wasn't sure what to do.

"No, I'll try really, really hard to keep my mouth open," she said with a wink. "I think you'll enjoy it if you decide to try it."

Milo nodded and crossed his fingers behind his back, hoping it would bring him all the luck in the world and help him to survive.

cHAPTER fivE

Mildred lifted her tongue from the grass and flopped it down again, closer to Milo this time, and he nervously climbed onto it with a little help from one of her enormous claws. He was surprised to learn that something as huge as Mildred could be so gentle and he wondered if her parents had taught her to be so tender and polite.

He was also amazed to find that her tongue was quite soft and dry. He wasn't sure why, but he was certain it would have been wet.

Mildred closed her mouth as she raised her head so that Milo wouldn't fall out. He thought it was like being in a lift and he wobbled a bit. Being in the dark and wobbling around was not a very nice experience, although it did remind him of a ride his parents had taken him on last summer at an adventure park.

Mildred finally opened her mouth and let out an enormous fire flame through her nostrils. The noise was the loudest Milo had ever heard in his life, like a clap of terrifying thunder and the noise of an aeroplane taking off, topped off with a bomb explosion. He could feel the cool air in her mouth and, sitting on her tongue, he gazed up at the stars above him. Wow! he thought, truly amazed by it all.

He was beginning to feel more relaxed in Mildred's company and thought he could trust her. Anyway, what other choice did anyone have if they were sitting in a dragon's mouth?

None at all, he thought.

"Milo," Mildred asked softly, "would you like me to fly around and see if we can find where you live? It's not very nice to feel lost, is it?"

"If you have your mouth closed so I don't fall out, how will I be able to see anything? And it's night time now, so I still wouldn't be able to see anything even if you opened it!"

"Mmmm. That's a very good point," Mildred said, scratching her very long chin with a claw.

Milo thought for a moment. "I *would* like to fly with you, though," he said. "It sounds super exciting!"

Mildred smiled. "In that case, I think it's time for you to climb up on to my back."

She lowered her head down to the ground and this time Milo held on to one of her tonsils to keep steady, causing Mildred to shriek in surprise. When she stopped moving, Milo crawled on his hands and knees to the tip of her tongue and sat down.

It took him quite a while but he slipped onto her chin and used her feathers to pull himself up onto her back. Mildred giggled with his movements, each one tickling her feathers, and as a result of her twitching and squirming Milo almost fell off a few times. But once he was safely on Mildred's back he snuggled into her, just before she shot another flame straight into the sky.

Most people think dragons are covered all over with very hard scales but, in fact, at the back of their necks are the softest feathers you'll find in the entire world.

"Wow!" Milo said. "I'm so high up I'd be able to see for miles and miles if the sun was out."

Mildred laughed. "Wait until we take off, Milo. In the light of the moon, you'll be able to see farther than you have ever done in your life."

Milo heard her take in an enormous breath of air and then she flung herself forwards and upwards, letting out a huge plume of flames. He felt both the cold air rushing past and the warm air heated up by the flames alongside him.

They climbed higher and higher in the darkness until Milo started to feel wet and he realised they were going through the clouds. He felt Mildred's heart below him beginning to beat faster and faster with the exertion of flying while she was taking in bigger and bigger gulps of air. The moon looked incredibly large and bright, making him squint, so he looked away and nestled further down into the warm feathers. And though it seems unlikely, because of all the excitement he was very, very tired and he fell into a deep and snuggly sleep.

cHAPTER six

When Milo opened his eyes he found himself staring at a rock face. It was no longer nighttime and he was peering out of a cave high up in a mountain. He could see the bright sun at the entrance although it was quite a long way away. Then he heard a low rumbling sound coming from behind him. Looking to his side he saw Mildred's vast shape, asleep. The sound was her belly rumbling. *I wonder what dragons really eat for breakfast,* he thought.

Mildred began to stir and stretched out her long body. She yawned so loudly that Milo had to cover his ears, and when she stopped he heard an almighty...

Milo fell flat onto his back and lay there for a moment, holding his breath, terrified that the cave was going to collapse on top of him. But it didn't. When he finally took a breath, two things happened at the same time.

1. He realised he couldn't move a single muscle, even though he tried.
2. He saw an enormous pink cloud floating up to the roof of the cave, which seemed to have come from Mildred's bottom!

"Ewwwwww! You farted!" Milo said, trying desperately to move his fingers so he could hold his nose, but he was frozen to the spot. And then suddenly, all he could smell was bananas! It was the most extraordinary bananary smell he'd ever smelt...like a bath full of banana custard, banana ice cream and banana milkshake all covered in chopped bananas and banana sauce. It was AMAZING!!!

Sitting up, Mildred said, "Morning, Milo. Oh. Did I do a pink?"

"A pink?" Milo asked. "If that means did you fart then yes, you did, and you nearly blew the roof off!"

Mildred laughed. "I'm sorry; I should have warned you I usually do one in the mornings. But you must admit it smelt rather nice! Did you notice you weren't able to move for a little while? That's to give everyone time to enjoy every single second of them, because they don't happen very often."

"My dad farts all the time," Milo said, "but they don't smell anything like bananas, so we don't freeze ... we just run!"

"Very sensible," Mildred said. "If I did a stinky pink, I'd run away too."

Milo giggled. "Why are they pink though? I'm pretty sure ours don't have a colour, but I'm definitely not going to look to find out."

"It's because of the food we eat. But don't ask me why they smell like bananas. There are dragon scientists all over the world trying to find out why. Anyway," she said, stretching her legs and standing up, "welcome to my home, Milo! Do you like it?"

Milo looked around. "It's a bit... empty," he said.

"We don't need much, just for the cave to be large enough for our friends to fit into comfortably, so we can spread out. We also need to be away from people because if a dragon snores the sound can travel for miles. And it's nice if the cave is dry so we can sleep on the floor. Over in that corner," she said, pointing, "I keep anything I think might be useful. Wood for fire, if I can't be bothered to blow flames with my nostrils, flowers to decorate with, especially white ones, and a store for leftover food. Talking of food, can I get you anything, Milo?"

"Could I have a drink, please? I'm quite thirsty," he said. Mildred nodded, and pottered around in the corner, preparing something for him. "It's a very nice cave," he told her, "but why did you bring me here?"

"After flying you around I could sense you were falling asleep, and as I don't know where you live I thought this was the best place to come. I have to hide in the day to make sure nobody sees me and, like you, I was very tired and needed to sleep. I hope that was alright."

Milo nodded and gave her a smile. Mildred brought back a piece of hollowed out rock that had some liquid in it. "Drink this," she said, as she offered it to him. "I hope you like it."

Taking the rock cup, Milo did what he always did when he was about to try and drink or eat something new: he put his nose over it and took a deep breath.

"Mmmm, it smells delicious. What is it?"

"It's pressed rose, buttercup, gooseberry, lavender, broccoli and minerals from the local lakes. Dragons make lots of it and keep it cool in the corners of their caves. We take it every morning to build up our strength. We also drink it when we feel sad which, luckily, is hardly ever."

Milo drank three cupfuls and immediately felt more awake.

"I know you come from England, Milo. Can you guess where I come from?" Mildred asked.

Milo thought for a moment, scratching his head. "I've no idea," he admitted.

'I come from Slovakia and that's where we are now," she said.

"Err, where's that?"

"It's a land located in what humans call Europe. It's a great place for dragons because although it's only a small country it has over six thousand caves, many where we can live. It has lots of mountains where we can fly and play in the snow without easily being seen, as well as many lakes with special minerals in them that help make us strong when we drink them."

"We're in a different COUNTRY?" Milo said, his eyes wide and his mouth hanging open in shock.

"We are! Is this the first time you've left England?"

"I've been to Wales, but that's all," he told her. He studied her huge face for a moment. "You look a bit sad, Mildred. Is there anything wrong? Would you like some of your drink?"

"Thank you, but I don't need a drink. This is my homeland and I miss it when I'm not here. So, for a little while when I come back, I feel a bit sad remembering how much it means to me. It's a very nice place and I'm very lucky to live here. Maybe you'll come back one day when you're grown up and explore all the non dragon places in the country." She smiled, and her tummy rumbled, which made all the pots and bowls and jugs wobble on their shelves. "Now I'm hungry so I'm going to go out and collect some food for breakfast. I won't be long."

"You're leaving me here ON MY OWN?" Milo shrieked.

"It'll be quicker that way. Just wait for me here and don't walk too close to the cave entrance. We're a very long way up!"

Milo watched as Mildred flew through the cave entrance and disappeared into the distance.

He couldn't help but worry about what he'd do if she never came back.

CHAPTER SEVEN

Milo needn't have worried about Mildred not coming back because she quickly returned to the cave holding the breakfast in her mouth. He was surprised and a little disappointed when he discovered what Slovakian dragons eat for breakfast. He was imagining eggs, bacon, fried bread and especially baked beans with brown sauce, but he was wrong.

Mildred had masses and masses of broccoli in her mouth. She didn't drop a single one, not even a floret. She kicked at the rock face inside the cave to make a perfect hole for a fire and cooked the broccoli with the flames from her nostrils. Milo felt the whole cave tremble when the hole was being made but he had already learnt that dragons often make loud noises and things *always* tremble, just like the ground he was standing on.

He almost fell over but was distracted by the wonderful smell coming from the cooking hole. Milo didn't like broccoli but had to admit it smelt amazing.

"The only time I've eaten broccoli was in Wales on holiday, visiting my Great Uncle Mark. He's my mum's uncle, but I just call him Uncle Mark, because it's easier. Anyway, the broccoli was disgusting," he said.

"It can depend on how it's cooked," Mildred said. "I don't like it raw. Why don't you try some? You must be as hungry as a dragon, and you did say how lovely it smelt!"

Milo screwed up his nose and shut his eyes tight as he was reluctant to try it. But he surprised himself as the broccoli was very soft and melted on his tongue. In fact, it was so delicious he went back and had another two portions before his breakfast was even finished.

"If you eat so much broccoli, why aren't your 'pinks' called 'greens'?" Milo asked."

"Ah, well. Most of the broccoli we eat is purple," Mildred told him.

"You can't get purple broccoli!" he said, sure she was making it up.

"Yes, you can! You should try it sometime, when you're back at home."

Home, Milo thought. It seemed such a long way away.

"I have a sister, Maureen, who used to live in Wales," Mildred told him. "I went there once and really enjoyed it. I wouldn't mind visiting again. Would you like to go and visit your uncle? What do you think?"

"I think I should be at school," Milo said softly. But then again, he wasn't sure what day it was. Maybe it was the weekend. "What day is it please?" he asked.

Mildred scratched her chin with one of her claws. "I really don't know. Dragons don't have days. We are either awake or asleep."

"How do you know what to do when you wake up then?" he asked.

"We always do the same things... we just fly about, explore, eat broccoli, sleep and play a lot of hide and seek," Mildred said.

Milo thought how nice it would be to not have any days at all, but be able to decide what he wanted to do whenever he woke up. But then again, he wondered how he would make friends with other children if there was no school. He was already missing Edwood. And how could he go to swimming club on Mondays if he didn't know if it was Monday?

Milo continued to think. If it was the weekend right now, he wouldn't get into trouble for missing school, because there wasn't any. He quite liked the idea of staying with Mildred until it was time to go home, but she didn't understand time, so he didn't know how he could ask. It was all very confusing. He was still thinking about his situation when Mildred spoke again.

"How often have you had the chance to visit your uncle in Wales on a *dragon?*" she said.

Milo laughed. "Well, never, obviously," he told her. "Can you speak any Welsh, Mildred? My uncle can!"

"Wrth gwrs y gallaf."

"What does that mean?"

She smiled. "It means, 'of course I can'."

Milo wondered how she knew Welsh if she had never even lived there. He was beginning to think that dragons might have special powers. After all, they could fly and make flames come out of their nostrils, and fart pink clouds. *Perhaps she has other powers, too,* he thought.

"Have you always been able to speak Welsh?" he asked.

"Yes. When a dragon learns something it's easy for other dragons to learn the same thing. We do this by looking at each other and concentrating until our thoughts become the same. So, I learnt Welsh from my sister, Maureen. I remember how she used to sing silently in Welsh for me."

"How did you know she was singing if she was silent?" Milo asked, laughing.

"Like I said, all dragons know what other dragons are thinking, so we could all hear her."

"But if you all know what you are all thinking all the time, doesn't it get really noisy?" He wondered what it would be like to hear Edwood's thoughts as well as his other friends' all at the same time. How would he concentrate?

"We can choose when we want to listen, Milo. We don't hear everything *all* the time. That would be quite exhausting!"

He decided that Mildred was not only very polite and gentle, but very clever and intelligent, and did indeed have special powers. He was curious about how many more he would discover.

"So, how about having a quick trip to Wales?" Mildred asked again.

Milo remembered going on long walks with his parents and his Uncle Mark in Wales when he was younger. They had always described Uncle Mark as eccentric, although Milo didn't really understand what it had meant. On one of these walks they had discovered and explored a really large cave. His parents recently told him that Mark had decided to go and live in this cave as a hermit. They told him that hermits enjoy living on their own, away from other people. He thought it would be a nice surprise for Mildred to learn that some humans enjoy living in caves as well.

"I think visiting my Uncle Mark is a fantastic idea!" Milo suddenly said.

"How wonderful!" Mildred replied, full of excitement. "Shall we go right now?"

Milo told Mildred the name of the town where Uncle Mark lived, and they took off as soon as she was sure nobody would see them.

chAPTER EighT

It took them 6 hours 43 minutes and 9 seconds exactly, flying above the clouds, to arrive in the area where Milo's uncle lived. They arrived at 3.05pm and because dragons generally only come out at night, Mildred suggested they needed to hide. Close by there was a big waterfall with a cave behind it that they swooped down into.

Mildred's nostrils started quivering and twitching as she smelt the air and she began to make squeaking noises as tears filled her eyes. She told Milo that she thought she recognised it as a cave that her sister had once lived in. She could tell by the smell. However, to Milo, it just smelt very musty and not very nice at all. As his eyes adjusted to the semi darkness, Milo realised it was indeed the same cave he, his parents and Mark had discovered years before, but now it appeared much bigger than he'd remembered it to be.

"Wouldn't it be incredible if my uncle and your sister knew each other?" Milo said. He looked at

Mildred and realised that she already knew the answer as she could read her sisters thoughts. *Dragons really are magical,* he thought.

After the long, tiring flight they slept in the cave until nightfall. Mildred had no trouble in sleeping but the mighty waterfall kept Milo awake and occasionally a spray of misty water found its way into the cave, waking him up, which he didn't like. Mildred seemed to enjoy the mist reaching her as Milo heard her purr in her sleep and occasionally turn over, shaking the cave, and him, for a few seconds every time.

Waking after a few hours, Milo was watching Mildred as she suddenly twitched her ears, opened her eyes and peered deep into the cave. He didn't know why but he understood he must stay silent. They could both hear voices close by.

"I'm sure I heard something over here," said a rasping voice. "Now remember, we must hunt down EVERY species of dragon in Europe for the Museum of Curiosities because once I have one from each species, I can collect the million pounds reward."

"We'll get our share as well, won't we?" said a big booming voice with a hint of terror in it.

The rasping voice continued. "Yes, yes of course you will; just you wait and see."

Mildred stopped breathing. Dragons can do that for up to 73 minutes at a time. She didn't want to be found by the dragon hunters.

Milo followed her example and stayed completely still until the two men turned round and moved away. The waterfall noise soon meant that they were safe to talk without being overheard. Milo realised that although Mildred was enormous and could explode flames out of her nose, she was really quite a shy and timid dragon. He was wondering what to say to her when they were both surprised by another voice.

"Who's there? What are you doing in MY cave?"

Mildred jumped in the air, frightened by the newcomer's voice, causing the whole cave to shake.

As a result, and as usual, Milo fell over. He was getting used to it now.

CHAPTER NINE

"Don't worry Mildred, this is my Uncle Mark!"

"And this is MY home!" Mark shouted, before the sound of Milo's voice had even hit his ears. He paused for a moment. "Is that really you, Milo? I haven't seen you for a few years but I never forget a voice! I don't see too well these days, I'm afraid."

Milo looked at his uncle and understood that he couldn't actually see at all, because his eyes were practically squeezed shut. Mark was a small, thin balding man with a very long beard. It was very difficult to guess his age and Milo realised he didn't know it either. Mark's clothes were a bit ragged and not very clean. His shoulders were hunched over, making him seem smaller than he really was. But his voice was booming, clear and strong.

"Yes, it's me, Uncle Mark! We thought you were one of those men who were talking about hunting dragons," Milo said.

"They're not very nice people," Mark said. "Stay away from them."

"Do you know them?"

Mark nodded. "I used to share this cave with a dragon. I didn't know she was here when I first moved in but one day I heard a soft sweet voice singing 'Sospen Fach', my favourite Welsh song. When the singing stopped I asked who was in the cave and that's when we started talking. I didn't realise she was a dragon due to my eyesight but we kept chatting and agreed to share the cave. That was very nice of her as she was here first. Then she told me she was a dragon. I was flabbergasted but not frightened, until she moved and I fell over as the cave shook. Then I realised how big and powerful she was, but I quickly got used to it.

"She was a lovely lady and helped me a lot. Because I couldn't see she would tidy up the cave, make fire with her nose to keep me warm, and fly off during the night and bring back all sorts of vegetables, but especially broccoli and lots of other lovely things."

"Your friends name is Maureen, isn't it?" Mildred said.

"Well I never! How did you know that?"

"She's my sister, and I can tell you that she's safe and well and definitely wants to return one day."

Mark took a deep breath. "I think she left because she was frightened after hearing those two men talking about hunting dragons. She told me she couldn't stay anymore but, like you said, she hoped to return sometime. She cried when she left. We used to get on so well, telling each other stories about our lives. I really miss her now."

Mark seemed very upset and Milo walked over to put his arm around him. Mildred plucked a feather from one of her wings and stroked him calmly.

"Maureen used to do that," Mark sobbed.

"I know," replied Mildred, Milo and Mark understanding that dragons know each other's thoughts.

"It's very nice of you both to comfort me," Mark said. "I'd really like to cook some dinner for you, if that's alright. I can't see, but I've learnt where everything is, so I shouldn't make too many mistakes."

"That would be wonderful," they both told him.

Mark had a food store that he kept in a corner of the cave away from the misty spray so everything would stay fresh.

"How about some roasted vegetables?" he asked. "Broccoli, of course, but also potatoes, beetroot, carrots, cabbage, celery and turnips."

He quickly built a fire, which Mildred lit very gently with a small flame from her nostril. The effort of doing this so gently brought on hiccups and each time she did it Milo and Mark fell over, until they realised it would be better if they just stayed sitting on the ground. Each hiccup bounced them a little closer to the cave opening where they were gently sprayed by the water from a nearby waterfall, which Mark quite enjoyed, having got used to it over the years. Mildred knew that Milo didn't like it so, in between hiccups, she gently shuffled him behind her, placing him on her tail feathers. Milo loved this as each time she hiccupped he got a ride on her tail as it went up and down. All three of them laughed as they waited for the next one to happen.

After the meal the light began to fade and Mildred got itchy feet and wings. It was time for her to exercise.

"Would you both like to come with me and fly around for a while?" she offered.

Mark explained that he regularly flew with Maureen and really missed the experience.

It wasn't long before they were soaring and diving over open countryside, along mountainsides and over lakes that they could only just make out as the sun went down. It was such great fun.

Mark and Milo were enjoying the soft feathers on the back of Mildred's neck, and the effect of the increasing darkness and the fresh air slowly soothed them, and they fell asleep.

Mildred needed much more exercise and decided to surprise them. She knew they would be asleep for hours, which gave her enough time to fly them to a very special place...

Dragon Land in Africa!

CHAPTER TEN

The best way to describe Dragon Land is as a massive playground for dragons, in the middle of a huge jungle. Only dragons are normally allowed to visit, but Mildred was certain that Mark and Milo would be welcome there.

Mildred landed and softly shook her feathers to awaken her sleeping passengers. She walked with them on her back to reception and asked for special permission for her two friends to stay, which was agreed by the dragon in charge. Mildred booked them all into a luxurious cave. Inside they found a piece of broccoli on each pillow, bottles of the finest feather conditioner and bottles of broccoli beer (a much sought after dragon's drink). There was also a special nostril brush.

Mildred picked up the nostril brush made of huge green fern leaves. She hadn't needed to use one for a long time but, now she thought about it, her nose was feeling a little bit tickly.

Holding the brush carefully between her claws she pushed the brush into one of her nostrils and twirled it around. Then there was even more of a tickle and she let out an almighty

aaaaaaaaachoo!

Mildred immediately felt better but was concerned to find Milo and Mark temporarily deafened by her sneeze and, of course, on the floor. After a bit of head shaking and ear slapping they both recovered and asked Mildred to warn them the next time she thought she might be about to sneeze. Or fart. Or do anything that would result in them ending up on their backs. Mildred nodded politely and apologised for not thinking about them beforehand.

"I always wondered what it would be like to be deaf," Milo said, "and it's not very nice."

"Although I can't see very well, my hearing is usually very good," Mark said. "I must admit, it quite frightened me to lose my hearing as well as my sight."

Mildred felt unhappy that she'd caused her friends to be uncomfortable and she made up her mind to do something about it later. She thought she could take them to the Broccoli Restaurant or the gigantic swimming pool. Then she had a great idea about something special she could arrange for Mark.

They returned to reception. Mildred asked where Maureen could be found and was delighted to learn she was staying in a cave close to theirs. She walked to her sister's cave with her friends on her back as flying was not allowed in this part of Dragon Land. After passing some of the attractions on the way such as the Broccoli Restaurant, the Broccoli Ice Cream Parlour and the Broccoli Sweet Shop, they arrived at Maureen's cave. She was sitting outside and using her claws to decorate the stone entrance with etchings. She didn't notice the three of them approaching.

"Hello, Maureen! Long time no see!" Mildred called out.

Now, when excited dragons meet each other they jump up and down and let out enormous flames of fire, which is exactly what Mildred and Maureen started to do. Mark and Milo were afraid of losing their footing as they knew the ground would soon be shaking beneath their feet. Milo had an idea and whispered in Mark's ear. They both quickly clambered from Mildred's back and onto the nearest tree, holding on tightly while the dragons greeted each other.

After a while Maureen lifted Mark on one of her claws, brought him up towards her gigantic face and blew gently on him. She knew he liked this and he responded by opening his arms and body into a cross shape so he could feel the full affect. Gently coming back to earth, Mark sat down quietly.

Mildred introduced Milo to Maureen. Together, the four of them sat down to eat a broccoli stew that Maureen had made earlier and wanted to share with them. Milo was changing his mind about broccoli and was determined to try other food he didn't like when he returned home.

I suppose I will return home one day, won't I? he thought.

CHAPTER ELEVEN

Maureen explained that since being in Dragon Land she had made lots of new friends, and she wanted the others to meet one in particular called Melinda.

"Hang on a minute! Do all dragon names begin with M?" Milo asked.

"Do all human visitors to Dragon Land have names that begin with M?" Maureen replied.

This made them all laugh but it didn't answer Milo's question. And when he thought about it, he didn't really care if their names did all begin with M anyway.

Melinda was an older dragon who had also lived in Wales many years ago, near the cave now occupied by Mark. She knew about the two dragon hunters because, she told them, they had caught her once. Everyone gasped in shock.

"It's alright," she explained, "they didn't hurt me. They just wanted my footprint, that's all."

"Why would they want that?" asked Milo.

"It's a strange thing, but humans love having competitions, especially ones with big rewards if

they win. They had entered a competition to win a lot of money if they found one. I think money lets you get lots of broccoli without having to pick it yourself."

"I get pocket money every week from my parents, which I buy sweets with. I wonder if they get the money from entering competitions," Milo said. Just for a moment he felt a bit sad and thought about his mum and dad and what they might be doing. He was beginning to miss them.

"On the day they caught me in my cave I had a cold and a blocked nose so I couldn't smell them or scare them with my fire," Melinda said. "I think they were quite brave to come near me, given I'm so big. They told me they'd heard me singing and realised I could talk. One of the men plucked up the courage to introduce himself, telling me his name was Terry. Both dragon hunters were clearly quite frightened and although they didn't realise it, so was I! I think we were all nervous but after talking some more I relaxed and asked them what they wanted.

"Showing me a map with lots of caves marked with the letter X, they explained about the competition they'd entered to find a dragon's footprint, and asked me if they could have the one I'd made in the mud outside the cave. Terry and Wayne, his friend, asked me how many different types of dragons there were and I told them there were many hundreds. Both left saying it was the first footprint they had managed to find, but they would keep on hunting for others."

Mildred shook her head, half-laughing. "So many times I've been frightened by hunters, but I never knew they only wanted footprints!"

"Maureen, why did you leave our cave and not come back?" Mark asked, turning to her.

"If I'd known they didn't want to hurt me I'd have stayed," she said sadly. But after they'd left I was frightened and wanted to talk to other dragons about any ideas they might have had to stop them hunting us, so I travelled here to Dragon Land. At the time my plan was to return very quickly but, as you can see, I'm still here. I'm so sorry. I missed you, Mark." She reached down and softly touched his face with the side of her claw, and he smiled.

"Is it true that humans believe dragons are extinct?" Melinda asked. "That's what the hunters told me."

"Most people believe that they never existed at all, and they're just made up," Milo answered. "I didn't know what to believe until I bumped into Mildred, and now I know you're real I think it's very strange that I'd never seen one of you before."

"Would you like to know what happened to dragons a long time ago? Why they stay out of sight and why you've never seen one?" she said.

Milo and Mark both nodded, and they settled down with their backs against a tree to listen.

CHAPTER TWELVE

"All the dinosaurs decided a long time ago to live here in the jungle, where there were no humans to hunt them or hurt them," Melinda began.

"I thought you were going to tell us about dragons, not dinosaurs," Milo said, with a puzzled look on his face.

"I'll come to that a bit later, Milo. The jungle was a big enough place for dinosaurs to live hidden away, and enjoy their lives. Despite their size and how they looked with big sharp teeth, long claws and flailing tails, they were really very shy animals who liked playing with each other more than anything. They pretended to fight and roll around playfully but no-one ever got hurt. They spent most of their time telling each other jokes ... mostly about humans," she added shyly.

Milo could tell she was far too polite to tell any of the jokes, even though he secretly wished she would!

"Some dinosaurs became a little bored and decided to explore outside the jungle. Dinosaurs hadn't flown for many years and the more adventurous of them decided to learn how to do it. Being shy, they only tried to fly at night and had to go to a different part of the jungle, because when they failed they woke up all the other sleeping dinosaurs with their heavy falls.

"Over time, some of this group grew wings and were able to fly successfully. These dinosaurs were named dragons, which means 'flying dinosaurs'. Does that answer your question, Milo?"

Milo nodded. "Can you tell us some more?"

"Of course! The dragons also taught themselves how to blow fire through their nostrils. This would be useful to see where they were flying at night as well as to frighten anyone who came near them; although many times in the beginning they burnt their nostrils and tongues and occasionally burnt other things like entire forests! Believe it or not, dragons are very careful about how they use their fire as they know how dangerous it can be when they are in the open. We always look up towards the sky so no-one gets hurt." With a broad smile, Melinda added, "They also discovered fire was very useful for cooking broccoli.

"Becoming more confident and curious, the dragons flew longer distances, discovering things they hadn't seen before like the sea, snow, mountains, deserts and people. They eventually travelled to all parts of the world but always at night so they wouldn't be seen. One of them discovered a cave, purely by chance when she didn't feel very well and couldn't fly. She rested in the cave for the night feeling safe and comfortable, and realised that it hid her from sight. She told the others about them. From then on, all dragons outside the jungle lived in caves during the day, but loved coming out at night. During their time in the caves they developed the ability to see in the dark which helped them stop bumping into the rock face and causing it to tremble. Some people who heard these bumps thought they were earthquakes!"

Maureen turned to Mark and said, "When I heard those men in our cave I got scared. Even though I realise they weren't going to hurt me, that doesn't mean other hunters won't. So I've developed an idea that I've been sharing with the other dragons, which will help us to live our lives safely, in the way we want to. My idea is that one night all the dragons from here in Dragon Land will fly to places all over the world, where very few humans live, and we'll create lots of footprints for them to discover. If they find them in these faraway places perhaps they will keep searching there and not bother us anywhere else. I talked with one dragon, Morticia, who is young and very cheeky. She thinks we should also leave some bum prints just to make the hunters wonder what they are!"

Milo sniggered. "That's a great idea!"

Maureen continued. "Mavis, an elderly and very wise dragon, is very concerned about the two hunters that saw Melinda and Maureen. She's worried they will tell other humans about us and we'll eventually be captured. She suggested we create fossils to try and convince everyone that all dragons are dead."

"What are fossils?" Milo asked.

Mark looked at him with a surprised expression on his face, as though he thought everyone should know what fossils are, and it made Milo feel a little bit silly.

But what Milo didn't know was that Mark had no idea what they were either and was really glad Milo had asked about them.

They all decided that Mavis was the best dragon to answer this question about fossils, and they invited her over to the cave to explain.

chAPTER THiRTEEN

"I heard hunters talking about fossils in a cave I was hiding in once," Mavis said, as she settled down between them. "The hunters had picked up some rocks and thrown them to the floor before they'd left. I cautiously picked up one of the rocks and turned it over, finding an impression of an ancient animal embedded in it. That's what a fossil is," she told them.

"Fossils might be of dinosaurs, insects, other animals, trees or flowers. Over millions of years as rocks are formed, the dead animals and flowers are trapped inside. When we find them can we see the fossils that are left by their imprints. Some look like the bones of animals and some others are footprints of animals, like dinosaurs."

"So how do we create fossils and convince people we are all dead?" asked Mildred.

"I've been working with Maureen and Morticia and we've been experimenting with rocks.

Morticia has used her incredible strength to firstly crush rocks into the shapes of dragon bones and to then blow holes into the ground ten metres deep and hundreds of metres long, which the bones are buried into. Then she fills the holes and presses everything back together again. She also walks up and down to create footprints and even the odd bum print! If we do this in lots of other places with the odd bone or print left on the ground for them to discover, we hope humans will spend many years searching for more. If we're careful to not be seen, the humans may think that just like dinosaurs, we are also extinct.

"Morticia had another wonderful idea and actually made some fossils of creatures that have never even existed. She thought this would be a good joke and that humans will think they keep on finding new species, which will make them search for more."

"Wow, what a great idea!" Mildred said. "I could make all sorts of bones and hide them. Maybe we could split whole cliffs if we pull together."

The dragons were become very excited, twitching, shuffling and blowing small flames up into the air. Suddenly, Maureen raised her tail and thumped it back down on the ground, resulting in everybody - including the dragons - falling over. She was signaling that dragons and people should listen more to each other.

"Maybe we could do this when there are terrible storms like hurricanes or floods or frightening gales of wind, so no one will hear us," suggested Maureen.

"I think you'd be safe in the desert as there are very few people that live there. Perhaps you could put some near the Pyramids in Egypt," Mark said. "I went to see them when I was younger and lots of tourists go there. If a dragon footprint was found I think they would search there for a very long time!"

"That's a great idea!" Maureen said. "Dragons love playing in the sand. We draw it up into our nostrils and blow it out, making sand rain. We also like digging gigantic holes and rolling down the sides of them. There are lots of games we could play while making and hiding fossils." Mark's suggestion was already exciting her.

"I have a question for you," Mark said, turning to Melanie with a very serious expression on his face. "How do dragons see in the dark?"

Mark always seemed to ask questions some time after he had been told about something. This meant his questions often appeared to come at strange times. Milo thought maybe this was what being eccentric meant, although he didn't like to ask.

"It's because of our enormous eyes, which are much bigger than anyone else's. It's why we can see small things a long way away, and why we can see through things, too."

"You can see *through* things?" gasped Milo.

"We can do all sorts of things that humans can't do but we're not supposed to talk about it."

"So you *can* do magic?" Milo asked, his eyes growing bigger as he got more excited.

"I can't answer that," Mavis said, smiling.

Suddenly everyone went quiet and Milo could feel that something important was going to happen, just like the time when his dog, Freya, was about to give birth to her puppies.

chApTER fouRTEEN

After what seemed like ages, Melanie raised herself up and pulled Mark gently towards her. She placed him on her right hand and lifted him up to her mouth. She whispered something in his ear that only he could hear, and then threw him high up into the sky, so high he couldn't be seen from the ground. After quite a few moments Mark floated silently back down and onto her feathers. Melanie twisted sideways and Mark dropped back down to his original place.

Nobody spoke for a very long time and they all stared at Mark. Milo didn't have any idea what was happening. "Are you okay, Uncle Mark?" he said.

Mark shook his head a few times, as if he was trying to flick water out of his ears.

"I feel a bit peculiar," he said, "but I'm alright, I think." And then he opened his eyes.

"I can see! My eyes work!" he shrieked.

He looked around at everyone and asked them to speak so he could match each face to a voice. He looked at the dragons and marveled at their magnificence. Then he started to cry, and everyone else cheered, and the dragons roared their flames high into the sky.

Milo couldn't believe what he had just seen, but then he hadn't believed in other things, had he? Like that broccoli could taste nice, or that he could fly on the back of a dragon. Mildred looked at him and understood his thoughts and how he was trying to make sense of everything.

"Don't worry, Milo, you will understand it all one day. Just try and enjoy it for now."

Milo smiled back and decided to do just that. He was happy for Mark, who had regained his sight, and for Melanie, who had helped him. He decided in future he would also help his friends whenever he could.

Mark spent the next day walking around Dragon Land and thanking all the dragons for what had happened. They all pretended not to know anything (as they were not allowed to talk about it). Mark understood and just kept grinning all day long, and looking at everything he came across. He noticed the insects on the trees, the clouds moving slowly in the sky, the colour of Milo's eyes, his dirty fingernails and much more. Often he stopped and just stared at something as though it was the first time he had ever seen it in his life.

Milo thought it was the same as the first time he had seen Mildred; he just couldn't stop staring at her. He realised that he often passed things without really noticing them and decided that he would start to look harder at everything if he had time. Wasn't it great that dragons could just decide what to do every day? *They always have time to notice things,* he thought.

Maureen, Mavis, Mildred, Melanie and Morticia called a meeting of all the dragons. It was an unusual affair as it took place high above the clouds, at night, with thousands of them flying around. They communicated by making circles in the air that only they understood, and it went on for exactly 37 minutes, the maximum time allowed for the meeting. By the end they had agreed a plan in response to Maureen's idea, which they would soon put into practice.

During this time Mark and Milo were asleep, but they were both having interesting dreams. Mark's dreams were about colours, all different kinds and shapes. He saw many different shades. Animals appeared, like purple lions and green apes, blue dogs and yellow and pink striped cats. Mark smiled, even though he was asleep.

Milo's dreams were about his home and Edwood. His parents were tucking him into bed as he was ill and Edwood had brought him some lemonade and toffee sweets. After a while Edwood lay on the bed and they fell asleep together side by side.

When he woke up, Milo had tears running down his cheeks and realised he was missing his parents, his dog, and Edwood. He wanted to go home but wondered how he could return.

CHAPTER FIFTEEN

The next day Milo and Mark watched as the dragons flew off to countries all over the world, where they then made thousands of foot and bum prints. Some were made in the Alaskan ice, others in the Sahara and Gobi deserts. More dragons flew to India, Russia and Canada. By the time they had finished there were prints in 102 countries that would take humans decades, if not centuries to discover.

After this they spent time creating the fossils that Mavis had suggested. Some fossils were made and dropped into peat bogs in Ireland. One dragon hid some in rocks near Niagara Falls, while others were forced into mountain ranges across all the continents. The more adventurous dragons flew deep inside volcanoes, placed the bones, and enjoyed the heat. Others went underwater and made them at the bottom of the sea.

Two days later when the dragons had returned, Milo talked to Mildred. He told her that he'd had such a fantastic time – the best time of his whole life – but that he really needed to go home.

"I understand, Milo, "she told him, as he squashed himself into her feathers.

Mark told Mildred that he wanted to return to Wales and, as he could now see, he decided he was not going to live in a cave anymore but try and move into a house. He wanted one where the sun would shine in through the windows and light up everything inside.

Mildred agreed to fly Milo and Mark back to their homes. "I must remember to give you both a special gift to remember me by," she said, with a tear in her eye.

Looking around him, Milo realised that all the dragons he had met were surrounding them both, ready to say goodbye.

They've read our minds, he thought to himself.

Dragons have an odd way of saying goodbye. They all fly up into the air at the same time and make a noise like a cross between a bee and a violin. Milo and Mark felt really drowsy as the sound encircled them, and they both fell into a very deep sleep.

Milo woke up in his bed at home. He looked around and everything was in its place, exactly how he had left it. His superhero books, monopoly game, catapult and football posters were looking back at him. His digital alarm clock was projecting the date and time onto his bedroom ceiling, and when he looked at it he rubbed his eyes in disbelief. It didn't make sense! When he'd had the argument with Edwood it had been Thursday, definitely Thursday, and his clock was telling him it was STILL Thursday, yet he'd been away for days! He'd lost count of the number of sleeps he'd had.

The dragons must have done some very clever magic, he thought.

He looked on his bed and under his bed and next to his bed for the gift that Mildred had said she was going to give him, but there was nothing there.

Disappointed, he padded downstairs, and when he saw his mum in the kitchen he raced towards her and gave her the biggest hug.

"I didn't hear you come in, love," she said. "Did you have a good time in the field with Edwood?"

"Uh....yeah," he said, still very confused about how it could still be the same day.

"Dinner's nearly ready," she told him.

"What are we having," he asked. He suddenly felt very hungry and his tummy rumbled in agreement. He tried not to laugh as he thought about Mildred's tummy rumbles, which had made him fall over so many times.

"I've made chicken, mashed potatoes and broccoli," she said. "And before you tell me, Milo, I *know* you don't want any broccoli!"

"Actually, Mum," he said, "I'd really like some today. A great big heap of it."

She stopped what she was doing and stared at him for a very long time before she spoke. "Okay... where is Milo and what have you done with him?" She took a step back and frowned at him.

Milo laughed and gave her another big hug, wrapping his arms around her waist. "I'm right here," he said. "I've missed you."

"Missed me?" She looked at the clock on the wall. "You've only been gone for an hour!"

At school the next day, Milo sat next to Edwood who was still not talking to him. Taking a big breath, he said, "I'm sorry I was mean to you, Edwood. Can we be friends again? I hate it when we argue, especially about silly things." Milo knew Edwood well and told him a few jokes he had learnt from the dragons, but didn't tell him that. Edwood couldn't help laughing, and they agreed a truce and promised each other that they would never argue again.

Milo asked Edwood if he would like to go to the library with him and see what else they could find out about dragons. Edwood shyly admitted he didn't really know a lot about them at all, and that his dad wasn't a scientist who studied them at the university. In fact, he worked at the hospital in the x-ray department, and studied people's bones.

"That's FAR more exciting! Milo told him.

After school, they walked together with their arms around each other's shoulders, happy to be friends again.

In the library they researched in lots of books and wrote down all the information they could find about dragons. Milo did this even though he knew a lot of it wasn't even true. He remembered Mildred's words about how it was strange that the two of them were arguing about something neither of them really knew much about.

Milo decided that being friends was far more important than *knowing* a lot. But he knew one thing … he wanted Edwood to be his best friend forever.

And he knew another thing, too… that he could never, ever tell anyone about his adventure with the dragons, because he needed and *wanted* to keep them safe.

Anyway, even if he did happen to accidently let his secret out, who in the world would ever believe him?

"*I would,*" his Uncle Mark said.

Milo spun around.

Uncle Mark wasn't in the library; he was hundreds of miles away in Wales. So how on earth could he have spoken to him?

And then Milo smiled, because he suddenly realised what the special gift was that Mildred had given them.

ThE ENd

ACKNOWLEDGEMENTS

I'd like to thank Elaine Denning for her editing and formatting, for introducing me to illustrating and other worlds previously unvisited, and for her ongoing support.

A big thanks to Rosie Quinn Harley for her brilliant and creative cover and illustrations.

Very special thanks to my lovely granddaughter, Lana, for all her encouragement.

Thanks to Carol Mayne and Sonia Dixon from my writing group for being the best sounding boards.

And finally... to my wonderful wife, Jeannette - thanks for putting up with me!

CONTACT

Author: philhampton@blueyonder.co.uk
Editor/formatter: www.elainedenning.com
Artwork: rosie.quinn.harley@googlemail.com

Printed in Great Britain
by Amazon

27016059R00050